Charles M. Schulz

Have Fun at Beanbag Camp!

HarperHorizon
An Imprint of HarperCollins*Publishers*

First published in 1998 by HarperCollins*Publishers* Inc. http://www.harpercollins.com
Copyright © 1998 United Feature Syndicate, Inc . All rights reserved.
HarperCollins ® and ♨ ® are trademarks of HarperCollins*Publishers* Inc. PEANUTS is a registered trademark of United Feature Syndicate, Inc.
PEANUTS © United Feature Syndicate, Inc. Based on the PEANUTS ® comic strip by Charles M. Schulz
http://www.unitedmedia.com
ISBN 0-694-00977-6
Printed in Canada.

"Well, Sally, what are you going to do this summer?"

"Nothing!"

"Nothing?"

"Not a thing!"

"This is going to be a beanbag summer!"

"I don't suppose you'd be interested in going to swim camp, would you?"

"Absolutely not!"

"Archery camp?
Boxing camp?
Tennis camp?
Hiking camp?
Music camp?
Church camp?"

"How about finding me a beanbag camp!"

"Well, you asked for it, and I did it.
I found you a beanbag camp."

"You're kidding!"

"All you have to do each day is lie in your beanbag and watch TV."

"Where do I sign?"

"Two weeks at beanbag camp! Nothing to do for two weeks except lie in a beanbag! This will be perfect!"

"Goodbye, big brother. I'll write if they give us time."

"Don't worry about it! Just relax and enjoy yourself."

"Is this the line for the bus?"

"Who's pushing?"

Dear Big Brother,

Life here at "Beanbag" camp is wonderful.
We don't do anything all day except lie in our
beanbags, watch TV and eat junk food.

Well, I have to close now and get this letter over
to the post office.

"... if I can get out of this beanbag."

"I got a letter from my sister Sally. She's at beanbag camp."

"All they do is lie in their beanbags, watch TV, and eat junk food."

"More potato chips, please!"

"I got another letter from my sister Sally. Here's what she says:

'I am still enjoying beanbag camp. All we do is lie in our beanbags, watch TV, and eat junk food. Sometimes they show us old movies.'"

"I'll bet Dorothy makes it home to Kansas!"

"That's right . . . Sally comes home today from beanbag camp. I'll be interested to see if she's changed."

"Sally! What happened?"

"Don't yell at me! What did you expect? All we did for two weeks was lie in our beanbags, watch TV, and eat junk food."

"Didn't you do *anything* else at camp?"

"Hang on to your hat . . . I signed up again for next year!"

"Oh no you don't! Stay away from that beanbag! You're through lying in that thing all day. You need to get outside and run around!"

"But what about my beanbag? Who's going to use it?"